# The Radish Day Jubilee

## By Sheilah B. Bruce
## Pictures by Lawrence DiFiori

*Muppet Press*
Holt, Rinehart and Winston
*New York*

Published by Holt, Rinehart and Winston,
383 Madison Avenue, New York, New York 10017.

Library of Congress Cataloging in Publication Data

Bruce, Sheilah B.
The radish day jubilee.

Summary: The Fraggles' plans for celebrating
Radish Day are superseded by plans to rescue Mokey
from the Gorgs, who are holding her prisoner while
she writes a ballad in their honor.
I. Di Fiori, Lawrence, ill.   II. Title.
PZ7.B82814Rad   1983      [Fic]      83-10805

ISBN 0-03-068678-4
First Edition

Printed in the United States of America
1 3 5 7 9 10 8 6 4 2

ISBN 0-03-068678-4

# Contents

# The Unsung Heroes of the Garden

IT was a quiet afternoon in Fraggle Rock, and Red Fraggle was wondering what to do. She'd already splashed in the pool, won first prize at the yo-yo meet, and practiced her new gymnastic trick, the singing somersault, until it was perfect. Now she felt like doing some serious playing. She looked around for her four best Fraggle friends—Gobo, Wembley, Boober, and Mokey—but they weren't in the Great Hall, and they weren't in the pool either. Come to think of it, Red hadn't seen them all morning.

"Maybe they're in Gobo and Wembley's room," thought Red, hoping they were up to something interesting. So she set off down the Long Twisty Tunnel, turned right at the Short Bumpy Tunnel, and skipped down The Tunnel That

Hums Sometimes. Yelling, "Hi, guys! It's me! Let's play!" she bounded cheerfully into the room.

And there were Gobo and Wembley and Boober, sitting at Mokey's feet with dazed looks on their faces. They looked as if they'd been put into a trance by whatever Mokey was reading from her diary.

"Hi, you guys," said Red.

"Hi," they answered together, never taking their eyes from Mokey's face.

"Hi, Red," said Mokey. "Come on in. I was just reading my new poem."

"It's really great," said Gobo admiringly. "Read it again, okay?"

"Yeah, Mokey, read it again," urged Wembley and Boober.

Mokey smiled. Then she read:

"Lords of the Garden, red and round,
Majestically sitting in the ground,
Grow grander and sweeter with each passing day,
And we'll sing your praises the fourth day in May."

"We are in the presence of a major talent," said Boober, shaking his head in awe. "Mokey can write a meaningful poem about anything—even radishes!"

"But you don't understand, little Boober," said Mokey, "radishes are very very important—they deserve praise and honor and song."

"Isn't there any more you can read us?" asked Gobo.

"Not yet," said Mokey. "Actually this is the very first part of a long poem I'm writing called *Ode to the Radish.*" Her eyes

got a dreamy, faraway look, a look that Red recognized. It meant that Mokey had a New Cause. "I've always wanted to write a poem about radishes," she said, "because they are truly the unsung heroes of the garden. When you think about it, they're awe-inspiring. They're pretty, they taste delicious, and no matter how many we pick, there are always more, just waiting for us. Isn't it amazing?"

Red liked radishes as much as the next Fraggle, but she couldn't understand Mokey's overwhelming enthusiasm.

"What do you mean about singing their praises the fourth day in May?" she asked.

"Mokey wants to have a holiday tomorrow called 'Radish Day'—in honor of radishes," explained Gobo.

"I don't know about you guys," added Wembley, "but I could really use a holiday. We haven't had one for three whole days!"

"Mokey's going to read her poem to everyone on Radish Day," said Gobo.

"Won't that be wonderful?" asked Wembley.

"Sure," said Red, feeling a twinge of envy. Then she had an idea. "Why doesn't each one of us do something in honor of radishes on Radish Day?"

"Yes," exclaimed Mokey, "something that shows our strong and deep commitment to this great vegetable of ours."

"Like what?" asked Boober. "I'm no artist. And I can't sing. All my voice does is scare baby Fraggles." He sighed.

"Little Boober," said Mokey assuringly, "there are all kinds of things you could do. Think now. Surely radishes have influenced your life in some remarkable way."

Boober concentrated so hard that his hat slid down onto

his nose. "Well, I did get a horrible stomachache once after I ate six of them," he said, brightening a little. "I could tell everyone about that."

"I knew you'd think of something," Mokey said.

"I've got a really terrific triple-backward-flip dive I could do," said Gobo. "I tried it for the first time after I ate a bunch of radishes. How about you, Red?" he added. "What are you going to do for Radish Day?"

Red's heart sank. She had been wondering the same thing. But she would never admit it to Gobo. She jumped up and said, "I'm going to do something really special and stupendous. And—creative! And artistic!"

"Oh yeah? Like what?" asked Gobo.

"I can't tell you yet. It's a secret that I absolutely cannot reveal." For a second Red wished that she could do something as easily and gracefully as Mokey. Like writing poems. Or painting pictures. "I—I'll tell you soon," she said. "Don't rush me." She thought, "I'd better come up with something fast!"

While all the other Fraggles scattered to put up signs about Radish Day, Red sat alone in Gobo and Wembley's room, glad for the moment that no one else was around. She had to figure out what to do for Radish Day, and she had a funny feeling it wasn't going to be easy. Just then her eyes fell on Mokey's diary, which was lying on the floor near Gobo's guitar.

Hoping that Mokey wouldn't mind, Red picked up the diary and began to leaf through it, looking at Mokey's many drawings and then reading her poem about radishes half aloud. She finished with a long sigh that was half admiring, half envious. "Wish I could draw pictures and write poems," she thought.

Red pored over one of the nicest drawings, a curly bunch of radish leaves emerging from the ground. It was Mokey's job to pick the radishes that the other Fraggles ate. The only problem was that the radishes grew in the Gorgs' Garden. Fifteen times the size of a Fraggle, the Gorgs were monstrous creatures who lived in a huge, ominous castle. Normally any Fraggle would think twice about venturing out into the Garden. But Red was getting really worried about what to do for Radish Day. Suddenly she had an idea. She jumped up. "Maybe if I went out to the Garden and stood in the radish patch, I'd be inspired, too!"

With Mokey's diary stashed under her arm for safekeeping, Red felt too excited to even think about feeling scared. She headed straight out to the radish patch, and that was where she saw it—already dug up—a radish so big, so red, and so round that it could have won a vegetable beauty contest. "Wow!" It came to her in a bright tingling flash that she could grab the radish, haul it back to her room, and carve it into a giant radish sculpture.

It was the best idea Red had had all day, so she took the radish by its bright green leaves and began to tug. In the process, she accidentally dropped Mokey's diary. But she was so busy with the radish she didn't even notice. "This'll make a great work of art," she thought as she dragged it out of the Garden. "Better than an old poem any day."

As she headed toward the Rock, Red had the nagging feeling that she'd forgotten something. But what? Then she remembered Mokey's diary. "Oh, no!" she thought. "I must

have dropped it!" Turning to go back, Red was met by the sight of Junior Gorg clumping along on Fraggle Patrol. "Whoops!" Red darted hastily behind a head of lettuce to ponder her dilemma. "I'll have to explain to Mokey what happened," she finally decided, "and then go back for the diary later when the coast is clear." Sheltered by the lettuce leaves, Red waited for Junior to look the other way. Then, quickly rolling the radish in front of her, she scurried home.

# 2

# Discovery

JUNIOR Gorg had been having a very bad day. First of all, his mother hadn't left him alone all morning. She'd kept him in the castle for hours, trying to teach him the proper way to announce the Royal Family. He'd been going half out of his mind with impatience. For one thing, he'd just set a new Fraggle trap, and he'd only been able to go outside twice to check on it. Torture.

"Repeat after me," Ma would say, for what seemed like the thousandth time. "Ladies and gentlemen of the court! Their Royal Majesties, the King and Queen of the Universe!"

Of course, there was no court, and there were no royal guests coming to the Silver Jubilee celebration Ma was planning. But she had it in her mind that if only Junior could announce the Royal Family correctly, someone would appear, like magic, to bow down to them.

To make matters worse, Junior could tell there'd been Fraggles in the Garden. There was a big new hole in the radish patch, a sure sign that the little varmints had been out there looting again. And he'd missed them because of his mother's yucky etiquette lessons! "GRRR!" Junior growled in frustration. Life just wasn't fair.

Outside at last, he kicked angrily at the ground, and an odd, square little pebble went flying. When it landed, it flipped open to show a white interior. Puzzled, Junior bent down to pick it up and, to his amazement, saw that it wasn't a pebble at all. It was a tiny, tiny book with even tinier little markings in it. Writing. And pictures! Junior was intrigued. Finding this minuscule book was the first interesting thing that had happened to him all day.

"Ma!" he bellowed. "Look what I found!"

Ma Gorg came running out of the castle, her tattered apron fluttering. "What is it, dear boy?" she asked, rushing to Junior's side.

He held the little book up for her to see, and she squinted at it. It was much smaller than her nose. "We need a magnifying glass," she said. "Fetch one, won't you, Junior dear?"

Junior lumbered into the castle and came back with a glass right away. Then he and Ma examined the little book together, as he held it and she turned the pages. They were so small that Ma had to concentrate very hard on grasping each one gently so that it wouldn't tear.

"Strange," said Ma Gorg, as she looked at the pages through the glass. "These seem to be drawings of radishes." Then she came to a page with writing on it. "What's this?" she murmured, frowning and reading it slowly. As she did, her eyebrows shot up in amazement, her cheeks turned bright red, and she gasped. "Junior," she cried. "Listen to this!" Then she read:

"Lords of the Garden, red and round,
Majestically sitting in the ground,
Grow grander and sweeter with each passing day,
And we'll sing your praises the fourth day in May."

Junior looked blankly at his mother. "I don't get it," he said. "What does it mean?"

"Why, this is a poem in honor of us!" exclaimed Ma. "The Lords of the Garden!"

"Well, what's all that stuff about singing praises the fourth day in May?" asked Junior. "Sounds pretty weird, if you ask me."

"Dear boy!" exclaimed his mother. "Don't you see? Our Silver Jubilee falls on the fourth of May! And this is a poem about it! It must have been written by a loyal subject, someone with a deep appreciation of our glorious past—and our brilliant future! I must tell the King about this!"

Turning toward the castle, she screeched "Your Majesty! Come quickly!" so loud that Junior winced and clamped his hands over his ears. A moment later, Pa Gorg emerged from the castle in his bathrobe, brandishing his royal sword, Gorgonzola. "Who dares attack? Stand back!" he shouted, peering around nearsightedly. Seeing no one but Ma and Junior, he bellowed, "Come forward! Stand and deliver! Who dares to threaten the Lords of the Universe?!" In his agitation he tripped over his half-tied shoelace and fell flat on his face.

His crown, which never sat very securely on his head, went flying into the radish patch.

Junior sighed. Pa was always falling all over himself in his attempts to catch the enemies of the kingdom. He was convinced that they lurked everywhere, just waiting for their chance to seize the last shreds of the once-great Gorg Empire. So Pa spent most of his days drawing up complicated battle plans, polishing Gorgonzola, and dusting his armor, which sat on a special platform in the royal dining room. "We must be ready for the Great Conflict," he would mutter darkly when his wife tried to coax him away.

Now Ma Gorg hoisted her husband to his feet. "No one is attacking, my dear," she told the King. "In fact, it's just the opposite. Someone is praising the Gorgs in verse, and getting ready to honor us on our Silver Jubilee!" She showed the tiny book to Pa, and as Junior slogged off dutifully to fetch the royal crown from the radish patch, he could hear his parents chattering away about the mysterious poet whose journal they had found. "Such sensitivity!" exclaimed his mother. "Whatever genius wrote this has a truly fine appreciation of the glories of Gorgdom!"

"Mmm, yes," agreed Pa, "sounds like a loyal subject to me."

"Poetry, humph!" snorted Junior, looking up and down the radish rows for his father's crown. "Who needs it!" He saw the glint of the crown behind a clump of radish leaves and started toward it. Then a slight movement nearby made him catch his breath and freeze. There was a Fraggle in the patch! And it was just about to step into his trap!

# 3
# Trapped!

MOKEY had often wished that she could fly. In the split second when Junior's trap went off and she flew into the air, she thought that somehow, miraculously, she had been given the gift. Then she realized what had happened. She had walked right into a trap. She was hanging high above the radish patch in a little net, while Junior Gorg smiled down at her with ferocious glee. He had taken her prisoner.

Mokey was terrified. She had been so upset, after Red sorrowfully told her how she'd accidentally dropped Mokey's diary in the Garden, that she'd rushed out to search for it herself. And once on familiar Gorg ground, Mokey was so distracted that she didn't even notice the trap until it went off. And now here she was, a prisoner! She was in a complete panic by the time Junior bellowed, "Ma! Pa! I caught one! A FRAGGLE!"

Mokey had seen Ma and Pa before, but only from a safe distance. The sight of them at close range, with Junior between them, was startling. Their faces, flushed with excitement and pressed up close as they examined her, were gigantic. They were near enough so Mokey could feel their hot breath and see every little bump on Pa Gorg's nose. She shrank back as they stared at her, and wished again she'd been more alert!

Junior was gleeful. "I caught it! I caught it! And now I'm gonna thump it!" he sang out.

"Junior, stop it!" protested Ma Gorg squeamishly. She could never understand her son's fascination with Fraggles. Whenever she saw one, she had the urge to jump up on a table and scream. They made her nervous. And who knew what kind of muck and dirt they were scurrying around in in that strange world of theirs? Ma wished they would keep out of the Garden. They were terrible pests.

Mokey struggled frantically to free herself from the trap.

"Yelch!" Ma shrieked. "Junior, get rid of that disgusting little thing!"

"Oh Ma," whined Junior, "I caught it. Why can't I do what I want with it?"

"Quiet," bellowed Pa. "Let's find out what this little grotesquerie is doing on our property. Ahem," he cleared his throat and turned to Ma. "Do these things speak or bark or what?"

"We speak," Mokey answered, gathering up all her courage. "We speak just like you do."

"Well, then, what do you think you're doing, trespassing in our Garden?" Pa roared. Mokey's lip quivered and she shook all over, but she was determined not to cry. "I was looking for my diary," she said as steadily as she could. "It's a little brown book. Have you seen it?"

Ma looked at Pa and Pa looked at Ma, and they both looked at Mokey and gasped.

"Our subject!" cried Pa.

"We must keep this Fraggle!" exclaimed Ma. "But even if it is a loyal subject, I don't want it in the house. Junior," she screamed at the top of her lungs, "bring out the royal bird-cage, on the double! We'll keep it outside, by the well. . . ."

The next thing Mokey knew, giant fingers were coming toward her through the webbing of the net. She backed away in fright until she saw what they held. A tiny brown book. Her diary.

*May 3*

*Dear Diary,*

*It's been the most awful day. First I lost you. Then I got captured by a Gorg! Usually we Fraggles are pretty good about avoiding traps, but I was so upset about losing you, diary, that I wasn't paying attention to anything else. Now I am a prisoner!*

*These Gorgs are the biggest things I've ever seen. They keep talking about this great empire they once had and how they used to rule the whole universe. But I'm not so sure. Pa hardly talks to me, and Ma doesn't seem all that bad. It's the one they call Junior I'm most worried about. Every time he looks at me, I just know he can't wait to get his big hairy hands on me and squash me. Oh, help! How will I ever get free?*

*But at least they gave you back to me, dear diary, and then*

they put me in a birdcage and told me I'd have to stay here and write a ballad for their Silver Jubilee. I never would have guessed the Gorgs were poetry lovers. Now all I've got to do is figure out what a Silver Jubilee is.

Love, Mokey

May 3, a little later

Dear Diary,

Well, it looks as if I won't have to write that ballad after all, because I won't be with the Gorgs much longer. That's what Red says, anyway. She sneaked over to visit me a little while ago, just as it was getting dark. I heard a loud "pssst!" from behind a cabbage, and there she was! Oh, it was so wonderful to see her, even though she took an awful risk to get out here.

Anyway, after I told her about my afternoon with the Gorgs, she said not to worry about being their prisoner. "Get ready to kiss your cage good-bye," she said. "I'm planning a foolproof escape that will get you back to the Rock in no time!"

Then she asked me how I got caught. I explained that I was looking for you, diary, and forgot to be careful. Red got very choked up about that. She thinks it's her fault because she left you out here. That's when she told me to leave it all to her, that she personally would make sure I escaped, or her name wasn't Red Fraggle. She's a real true-blue friend.

Well, good night diary. I'm very scared and awfully glad you're here to keep me company.

Love, Mokey

# 4
# Appreciation

LIKE all his friends, Wembley was miserably worried about Mokey. She'd been the Gorgs' prisoner all day and no one, not even Gobo, had come up with a good escape plan for her. Even though Red kept saying, "Just leave it to me, I'll think of something," Wembley wasn't convinced that she would. The situation was extremely dangerous. After all, Mokey's life was at stake! She was locked up in a cage at Junior Gorg's mercy! Wembley was disappointed that Gobo, the Fraggle he admired most, hadn't thought of a solution yet. But now he knew, with no time to waste, that there was only one other creature with the brilliance, the wisdom, and the sheer sense to help everyone out of this mess. He had to see the Trash Heap, even if it meant risking his own life to get to her.

Visiting the Trash Heap was dangerous because she lived in a little clearing in the woods behind the Gorgs' castle. And if one of the immense, horrifying Gorgs was around, it made the trip to see her a fur-raising experience. But Wembley was feeling desperate. So he took a deep breath and took off. Sneaking into the Gorgs' Garden, he pulled up the best-looking radish he could find. The Trash Heap would like that. Then he zigzagged past the castle at lightning speed, tumbled through the flower patch, over the wall, and into her clearing.

"Approach the glorious Trash Heap," sang Philo and Gunge, her two faithful attendants. "All-wise, all-knowing, all ears."

"Hello, Madame Trash Heap," said Wembley, breathless as he stepped forward. "I've come to ask your advice. And I've brought you this." He offered her the radish.

"Why, sweetheart, how nice of you!" The Trash Heap popped it into her mouth and crunched on it loudly. Then she sighed with satisfaction. "What a delicious raspberry."

"Radish," corrected Wembley.

"Never mind," said the Trash Heap, "it's the thought that counts. Now what would you like to ask me?" She adjusted her hairdo, a complicated arrangement of dried flowers, steel wool, wood shavings, and banana peel.

"It's about my friend Mokey," said Wembley. "She's been captured by the Gorgs! They've put her into a cage and they're keeping her there and forcing her to write some kind of ballad for them. It's terrible! We want to get her out, but no one can think of how to do it. Can you help us?"

The Trash Heap settled down a little, rearranging a few strands of spaghetti on her lap. She was quiet for so long that Wembley thought she had fallen asleep.

Then, suddenly, she said, "Mokey? Mokey? Is she the purple one?"

"Well, more sort of pink," said Wembley.

"Oh, the one with the lovely sweater? The poet?"

"That's her."

"I remember," said the Trash Heap. "She even wrote a
poem for me once. Let's see if I can remember it. . . ." She
closed her eyes and then recited:

> "Kindly eyes
> Wisdom deep
> Friendly ears—
> The Trash Heap!"

Philo and Gunge clapped and whistled, and Wembley
blinked back a tear. Mokey really *was* a good poet. "But
Madame Trash Heap," Wembley said, "what does that have
to do with helping her escape? I mean, she's stuck there and
she's in terrible danger, even if she is a good poet."

"Her poetry can help her escape, and it could do something
for the Gorgs, too," said the Trash Heap. "As a matter of
fact, it could do a lot for the Gorgs." The Trash Heap smiled.
Then she leaned forward and patted Wembley on the hand.
"Thanks for the ravioli, dearie. Everyone likes to be appreciated once in a while. I know I do." Then her eyes closed
and she was still.

"The Trash Heap has spoken!" Philo and Gunge turned
to Wembley, their faces stern.

"A precipitate onset of severe fatigue," said Philo. "Yeah,
she's tired," said Gunge. "You'd better go."

Feeling very bewildered, Wembley made his way back home. Red was where Wembley had left her, sitting in a corner in Mokey's room. Gobo and Boober were there, too. All of them were frowning.

"Hi, guys," said Wembley.

" 'Lo, Wembley," said Red. "Where've you been?"

"To the Trash Heap. I asked her what we should do about Mokey."

"What'd she say?" they all asked at once.

"She said Mokey's poetry could help her escape and could help the Gorgs, too. And that everyone likes to be appreciated once in a while."

"I don't get it," said Gobo.

"Me neither," said Boober and Red. They all thought for a minute.

"Hold it!" shouted Gobo. "Maybe she means that if Mokey writes a ballad for the Gorgs, it'll help them feel appreciated, and then they'll let her go!"

"Can you see a Gorg ever letting a Fraggle go?" moaned Boober.

"Wait a second, you guys!" cried Red. "The Trash Heap is right! We might be able to appreciate the Gorgs! And Mokey's poetry *might* help everyone!"

"But they're our enemies," said Wembley.

"They'd eat us for breakfast if they could!" cried Boober.

"You're crazy!" said Gobo.

"I'm not crazy," said Red, hopping up and down with excitement. "I've got a plan! A terrific plan."

"If it has anything to do with telling the Gorgs how great they are, you can count me out," said Gobo.

"In a way it does," said Red. "Wait—wait!" she yelled over the chorus of groans. "I'm talking about tricking them! Now listen—it'll be a cinch! First we get Mokey to tell the Gorgs she's written the ballad for them, and that she'll read it for their Silver Jubilee."

"Why would she do a thing like that?" asked Boober with a shudder.

"Because they told her to, and then *we* can all go out there and be the audience—"

"Go out to the Garden, in the open? No way!" said Boober.

"They'd thump us in a minute," added Gobo.

Wembley shook his head dubiously. "I don't know . . ." he began.

"You don't understand!" cried Red. "Once we're out there with the Gorgs, we can spring into action. We can outwit them and outfox them and outrun them and—"

"I get it!" interrupted Gobo. "You mean once we're all out there, we can rescue Mokey!"

" 'Course," said Red. "We'll get Mokey to charm the Gorgs into calling a truce. For, say, one hour, Gorgs will be at peace with Fraggles—no chasing and no thumping. They'll invite us to be their guests at their Silver Jubilee, so we can go into the Garden safely. Then after Mokey reads her poem, I'll give the signal and we'll all run in different directions. That'll distract the Gorgs and give us time to get Mokey out of her cage to escape!"

Red's friends thought it over.

"Listen, guys," Red pleaded, "we have to do *something!* Mokey's in terrible danger!"

"You know, it just might work," said Gobo.

"We're all doomed anyway," said Boober.

"I just know it'll work," cried Red, jumping up and down.

"Sounds good to me," said Wembley, agreeably.

"Now, when we're in the Garden," Red added, "we'll need a special signal to mobilize the escape. I can cry—"

"Give me Fragglehood or give me death!" proclaimed Gobo.

"Perfect!" cried Boober, Wembley, and Red.

"Now, let's get organized! May fourth is tomorrow," said Red. "I'll sneak out to see Mokey right away to tell her the good news. She'll be a free Fraggle in no time!"

# 5

# Our Own Personal Poet Laureate

WHEN Red came creeping up to Mokey's cage, Mokey was writing furiously in her diary, trying one poem after another. She still couldn't come up with the right ballad for the Gorgs.

"Red! Oh, I'm so glad to see you," said Mokey. "I've been so scared. You've got to get me out of here!"

"We're going to get you out of here—tomorrow! But you've got to help!" Red described the truce and escape plan to Mokey, ending with "So all you have to do is get them to call a truce and invite us. We'll do the rest!"

"Why should they want to invite the Fraggles? They hate Fraggles," said Mokey.

"But they need loyal subjects," said Red. "How can they have a ballad-reading without an audience? It wouldn't be any fun. And besides, we're all they've got!"

"I guess so," said Mokey. She frowned. "I haven't even written the ballad yet. I can't figure out what a Silver—"

"You've got to write this poem, and you've got to make it good," said Red. "Just get them to promise they'll keep the truce until you're finished. And you be ready for the signal."

Suddenly Mokey and Red heard the sound of slow, heavy footsteps. It was a Gorg.

"Quick! Run away!" said Mokey.

"Don't forget," said Red. "I'll say 'Give me Fragglehood or give me death!' And don't worry!" Red darted away.

A moment later, Ma's enormous face peered at Mokey through the bars of the birdcage.

"Good evening, Your uh, Queenness."

"It's Highness."

"Oh, well, um, good evening, Your Highness."

"Finished with the ballad for tomorrow?" asked Ma, glancing at the diary in Mokey's lap.

"Well, no," said Mokey. "As a matter of fact, I haven't written it yet."

"WHAT??" Ma screeched so loudly that the bars of the cage rattled. "WHY NOT???" Her face reddened and her eyes glinted menacingly.

It was the first time Mokey had seen Ma act as mean as Junior. She looked terrifying. "Because I don't know what a Silver Jubilee is," Mokey said, as evenly as she could.

"But why didn't you ask? There's so little time! And it's such an important occasion! The Silver Jubilee is the twenty-five thousandth anniversary of Gorg rule!" Ma drew herself up to her full height, so that Mokey had to crane her neck to see her. "Imagine!" she said proudly, "thousands of years

of wise, kindly, but masterful leadership over all of . . . this!"
She gestured grandly over the vegetable patch in the direction of the Gorgs' castle. "It's a high point in Gorg history!"

"Yes, well I can see that now," said Mokey.

"Good," said the Queen, "because I knew, the minute I read your wonderful poem about us, that you and only you could write about our Silver Jubilee the way it deserves to be written about. With brilliance, sensitivity, and genius. Even if you are only a Fraggle."

Mokey was confused. "Excuse me, Your Highness. A poem I wrote about you? What poem? Where?"

"In your book, loyal subject," said the Queen. "The one that goes . . . " And here she recited from memory:

"Lords of the Garden, red and round,
Majestically sitting in the ground,
Grow grander and sweeter with each passing day,
And we'll sing your praises the fourth day in May."

"Oh, that one!" said Mokey, astonished to realize Ma's mistake.

"Yes, that one," said Ma. "It's a masterpiece!"

"Your Highness! It doesn't really deserve such praise—"

"Oh, but it does," said Ma. "It treats its subjects—us—with all the respect we have always deserved from *our* subjects—the rest of you. And even more important, it proves that ancient Gorg prophecy is about to be fulfilled!"

"What's that?" asked Mokey.

"That a great poet will immortalize us for all time," said Ma, her eyes lighting up. "A weaver of legends, a rhymer of noble rhymes, a fitting addition to the once and future glories of the Gorg royal court. In other words, our own personal poet laureate—you!"

"What?" asked Mokey, her eyes wide.

"I know it's no accident that you've come to us on the very eve of our Silver Jubilee," Ma continued. "No, the mysterious forces of the universe are at work! Destiny has brought you here. And here is where you will stay—forever!"

"But I want to go home," Mokey said, fighting back tears.

"This will be your home!" Ma said, oblivious to Mokey's feelings. "You will be our royal poet. And the Gorgs will be restored to their former greatness!" Ma straightened her crown, mopped her forehead with her tattered lace handkerchief, and fixed Mokey with a baleful eye. "So you'd better get to work on that ballad, and quick!"

*May 3, even later*

*Dear Diary,*

*I've never been so scared in my life! The Gorgs want to keep me here as their slave! And what if this escape plan of Red's doesn't work? Then the Gorgs will get us all!*

*Meanwhile, I have to somehow convince them to invite the Fraggles to the celebration so I can be rescued. So now I have to finish this ballad. Oh, how can I write anything good about Gorgs?*

*But I do have one secret for you, diary, and I hope you never reveal it. I really liked being called sensitive and brilliant and a genius. Even if it was by the Gorgs.*

*Love, Mokey*

# 6
# Fraggles to the Rescue

B<small>Y</small> the next morning Mokey had finished her ballad. So when Ma Gorg came out to her cage, she was finally ready to propose the truce.

"Good morning, poet subject," Ma said.

"Good morning, Your Highness," Mokey answered. "I've finished the ballad."

"Excellent," said the Queen. "Let me see it."

"Oh no," Mokey said. "I'm saving it for this afternoon's celebration. In fact, I've been meaning to talk to you about that."

"Yes," Ma said.

"Well," Mokey continued, fumbling for the right words, "well, for this great and glorious occasion, I think you should have a huge and wonderful audience. Lots of loyal subjects to pay their respects to the grand and great Gorgs."

"That's a divine idea," said the Queen, "but I haven't seen any loyal subjects in the neighborhood lately."

"Well, I have," Mokey said, "and they're my friends. So if I invite them, they'll come. There's just one problem. . . ."

"Yes?"

"Well, they'll only come if the Gorgs promise to call a truce and not to chase or thump them for one hour."

"Your wish is granted!" exclaimed the Queen. "You provide the audience, I'll provide the peace. Oh, this is thrilling! More loyal subjects! Just wait till I tell His Majesty!" With that, the Queen toddled off toward the castle, returning moments later with the King and Junior.

"All right, Junior, go ahead," she said.

Standing at attention, Junior Gorg unrolled a hastily scribbled scroll and read aloud: "This royal proclamation royally proclaims that the grand and glorious Gorgs declare a truce with all their loyal subjects to last for one hour during today's Silver Jubilee celebration. Signed, the King and Queen of the Universe."

"Oh Ma!" Junior whined. "I hate truces!"

"Too bad, Junior," Ma said. "Now go and polish our crowns. This is going to be a big day!"

Meanwhile, back at Fraggle Rock, Red was getting ready to lead the Fraggles on their great mission to rescue Mokey. She had her whistle around her neck and was doing some last-minute preparation in her room. "Forward, march!" she cried, blowing the whistle and doing a triple somersault. "Head for the Rock!" she called out for practice, blowing the whistle again and turning a dazzling double backward flip. As she landed, dizzy and triumphant, she heard the sound of slow clapping.

"Not bad," said Gobo from the doorway. "But I thought you were leading a rescue, Red, not a gymnastic meet."

"Just you wait, Gobo. These commands will make the rescue go like clockwork."

"What about the Gorgs?" Gobo asked.

"Mokey's getting them to call a truce," Red answered. "In honor of their Silver Jubilee, the Queen is giving her solemn promise that no one will get chased or thumped—for at least an hour. So let's get organized! We don't have much time! You get Wembley and Boober and I'll sound the call for assembly. See you in the Great Hall in exactly two minutes." With that, Red whizzed down the Long Twisty Tunnel, took the Thirty-nine Steps in three leaps, and bounded into the Great Hall, the official Fraggle meeting place and playground. The Hall was so big that ten thousand or so Fraggles could fit into it at once. As soon as Red arrived, she blew three thundering notes on the mighty Fraggle horn. This was the signal for an Important Meeting.

Within two minutes the Hall was filled with Fraggles. There were the Elder Fraggles, the Baby Fraggles, the Ever-Expanding Fraggle Chorus, the Fraggle Boardgame Buffs, the Fraggle Tap-Dancing Team, the Yo-Yo Experts, the Fraggle Jingle Band, and the Omnipotent Venerable and Eminent Council of Sages. The din they all made was tremendous. A great roaring swell of "FRAGGLEFRAGGLEFRAGGLEFRAGGLE" filled the air, and Red had to blow her whistle eleven times before the noise died down and the Hall was quiet.

"Fellow Fraggles," she cried, "this Important Meeting has been called for a very important reason. The rescue of Mokey Fraggle!!!"

Squeaks and murmurs of interest rippled through the Hall.

Red blew her whistle for quiet. "I will now demonstrate the procedure for the rescue," she announced. "When I give the first signal" and here she called "Forward, march!," blew her whistle, and turned a triple somersault—"we will march out to the Gorgs' Garden and seat ourselves in rows. Orderly rows!" The Elder Fraggles nodded their approval. "Mokey and the Gorgs will be waiting for us," Red continued, "and the Gorgs have called a truce—one hour of peace with the Fraggles. Now, when we arrive, Mokey will come forward to read her ballad." Red paused dramatically. "As soon as she is finished, I will shout, 'Give me Fragglehood or give me death!' And the moment I do, all Fraggles will break up into three large groups—one led by Gobo, one led by Wembley, and one led by me. We will run away from the Gorgs in three different directions, calling 'Fragglefragglefragglefraggle' as loudly as we can. This will confuse the Gorgs. They will chase us, and we will help Mokey escape! Then all we have to do is run back to the Rock ourselves." Red blew her whistle, called out several commands, and finished her demonstration with a perfect double backward flip.

There were gasps of admiration from the crowd.

"Are we ready?" she yelled.

"Ready when you are!" called Gobo. Then a great Fraggle cheer went up. The Fraggle Tap-Dancing Team began to hop and bounce eagerly and the Fraggle Jingle Band launched into a rousing march. With a deafening blast on her whistle, Red

called "Forward, march!" and tried to turn another triple somersault, and the Fraggle rescue mission was on its way.

Wembley was doing his best to keep the stragglers in line at the rear of the crowd when he felt a pat on his shoulder. It was Boober, whose mournful face looked even longer and sadder than usual. "Hey, pal," he said, patting Wembley again, "I hope we get out of this alive. I sincerely do. But I doubt it."

"Don't worry, Boober," said Wembley, feeling the icy chill of fear himself. Red had told them the Gorgs had called a truce, but who could help worrying? Could anyone really trust Junior to lay down his club, even for an hour? Wembley sighed. Only yesterday he'd been worrying because he couldn't think of anything to do for Radish Day. And now here he was, on a Radish Day everyone else had forgotten, faced with a task so dangerous it made his visits to the Trash Heap seem downright silly.

Wembley and Boober paused for a moment just as they reached the entrance to the Garden. Then each tied a double good-luck knot in his tail and started in.

# 7
# The Radish Day Jubilee

RED, who was leading the Fraggles, marched into the Garden as steadily as she could, but it was all she could do to keep herself in line. She prickled with desire to zigzag off, screaming "FRAGGLEFRAGGLEFRAGGLEFRAGGLE" at the top of her lungs, leading the Gorgs on a wild-goose chase they would never forget.

But she restrained herself. She had work to do. First she got the Tap-Dancing Team to stop dancing and sit down. Then she convinced the Yo-Yo Experts to stop looping the loop and put their yo-yos away. After that, she rounded up a group of Toddling Fraggles who were playing hide-and-seek in the Garden's zucchini vines. Finally Red took her own seat in front of the area where the Gorgs and Mokey were waiting. The Gorgs, she noticed, were dressed in their finest

clothing. The King wore a purple velvet robe, the Queen's gown was trimmed with lace, and even Junior, pulling at his shirt collar irritably, wore a red silk tie with his overalls.

When the Fraggles were finally seated, the King and Queen stepped forward to look over their audience. "It's all Fraggles," said the King. "Where are our other loyal subjects?"

"I'm sure they'll be here," said the Queen. "We'll just have to wait."

Some time passed, and both the Fraggles and the Gorgs were getting restless. Finally Mokey had an idea. "Your Highness," she called from her cage, "you know, of course, that my poem must be read just as the sun is at its highest point over the Garden. You know, 'highest' for 'Highness' and everything."

"Oh, uh, yes, naturally I know that," said the Queen, who knew no such thing. "Yes, all right, I guess we can't wait any longer then. We shall begin."

The King cleared his throat. "Ladies and gentlemen," he said. . . . Then he remembered the audience—all Fraggles. Well, he thought, Fraggles are still better than nothing. "Ladies, gentlemen, and Fraggles," he said, "we are gathered here today to celebrate an important—"

"—and a great . . ." said Ma.

" . . . an important and a great, ah, day in our history. This day—"

"This important, great, and unforgettable day," prompted the Queen.

" . . . marks the twenty-five thousandth anniversary of our rule!" said the King quickly, before his wife could interrupt him again.

"Our Silver Jubilee!" she finished, looking at the audience of Fraggles expectantly. There was a long silence. Then Mokey, who understood what the Queen was waiting for, began to clap politely. The Fraggles followed her example, and before long, waves of applause swept over the Garden. The Queen's face flushed with pleasure. As soon as the applause died down, she said, "And now, to read a ballad especially written for this great day, I call on our poet laureate—Mokey Fraggle!"

The Fraggles cheered, whistled, and squealed excitedly, and a group in the back chanted "M—O—K—E—Y!" at the top of their lungs.

Red noticed that the commotion was affecting Junior, who was frowning darkly and shifting in his chair. "Shhh!" she called. "Quiet down, everyone!" Remembering that they were to wait for Red's signal, all the Fraggles fell silent at once. Suddenly, the Garden was absolutely still.

Red, poised to jump at any second, tingled with anticipation. The escape would soon begin!

Mokey looked out over the audience solemnly. Then she opened her diary. "This is a ballad for the Gorgs," she said.

"Long ago in days of old
The Gorgs ruled everywhere.
Their power it was grand and great,
Their leadership was fair.

Their subjects all admired them so
Their royal court was gay;
Their royal hearts were well content
From day to shining day.

They thought they'd rule forevermore.
Alas! They were mistaken.
One day their empire toppled down,
Their power it was shaken.

Now their empire is a garden patch
Where they plant and seed and hoe,
And their subjects are root vegetables
That they command to grow.

And the royal Gorgs are gay no more
For their days are not carefree.
So we wish them dreams of better days
On their Silver Jubilee—
Yes, we wish them many golden dreams
On their Silver Jubilee!"

Mokey closed her diary and the Garden was once again absolutely still. At last, after what seemed like forever, Pa began to applaud, and Junior followed dutifully. "Splendid!" bellowed Pa. "Truly worthy of the glories of Gorgdom!"

Suddenly a loud tearful wail came from Ma Gorg. She was furious. "Oh no!" she cried. "You fools! That was the most hideous poem I've ever heard!" With tears coursing down her cheeks, she rushed over, picked up Mokey's cage, and began to shake it. "How could you say our empire toppled down?" she hissed, glaring at Mokey. "We are still the Rulers of the Universe, you little rat! I hereby declare the Gorg and Fraggle truce . . . over!!!"

Junior Gorg leaped to his feet as if awakening from a dream.

Sweat glistened on his massive forehead, and there was a strange, dark glimmer in his eyes, as if seeing so many Fraggles so close had unhinged his mind. Red's heart stopped beating for an instant when she saw that he was holding his giant club behind his back. She gasped as he ran forward, brandishing it.

But fortunately for the Fraggles, the Queen turned at the same moment, and Junior's charge brought him thudding right into his mother. She screamed, staggered, and dropped Mokey's cage to the ground. With a bellow of pain and frustration, Junior fell back on the ground, his club flying out of control and hitting the castle's kitchen window with a loud, splintering crash.

Enraged, the Queen turned on her son, and it was all the King could do to keep her from kicking him. "My dearest,

control yourself!" he cried, blocking her so that her foot landed on his shins instead. "Owww!" he yelled, backing away.

Junior bellowed again and tried to get to his feet, but the Queen would not let him. She planted a foot on his chest and screamed, "Can't you learn any manners, you overgrown turnip? Even if Fraggles can't behave, you should! Oh!" she wailed miserably, "this was supposed to be a *really* Proper Ceremony!"

As the Gorgs squabbled, the Fraggles sprang into action. Red finally realized this was the moment she had been waiting for all day. She blasted on her whistle, turned a perfect double backward flip, and screamed, "Give me Fragglehood or give me death!" as loudly as she could. All the Fraggles jumped to attention at her signal, and with a mighty chorus of

"FRAGGLEFRAGGLEFRAGGLE!" they began to scatter and run toward home.

Red ran over to Mokey, opened the cage, and took her hand. "Let's get out of here," she said urgently, "on the double! And hang on to your diary, okay?"

Mokey nodded, dazed from all the excitement. Through the Garden, through the radish patch, and past the castle the pair ran. Both of them were breathless by the time they got back to the Rock.

"Oh, Red," Mokey gasped. "I've never been so glad to see my friends in my life! You all risked your lives for me, and I'll never forget it!"

"You risk your life for us every time you go into the Gorgs' Garden," Red said. "Anyway, friends are supposed to take care of each other."

Gobo, Wembley, and Boober had gathered round by this time, and the Fraggle Five gave each other big hugs. "Welcome home, Mokey," the others said. "It's great to have you back."